EMMA AND THE MAGIC DANCE

Written and illustrated by LOU ALPERT

Whispering Coyote Press Inc./New York

Published by Whispering Coyote Press Inc.
P.O. Box 2159, Halesite, New York 11743-2159
Text copyright © 1991 by Lou Alpert
Illustrations copyright © 1991 by Lou Alpert
Printed in the United States of America
ISBN 1-879085-01-1

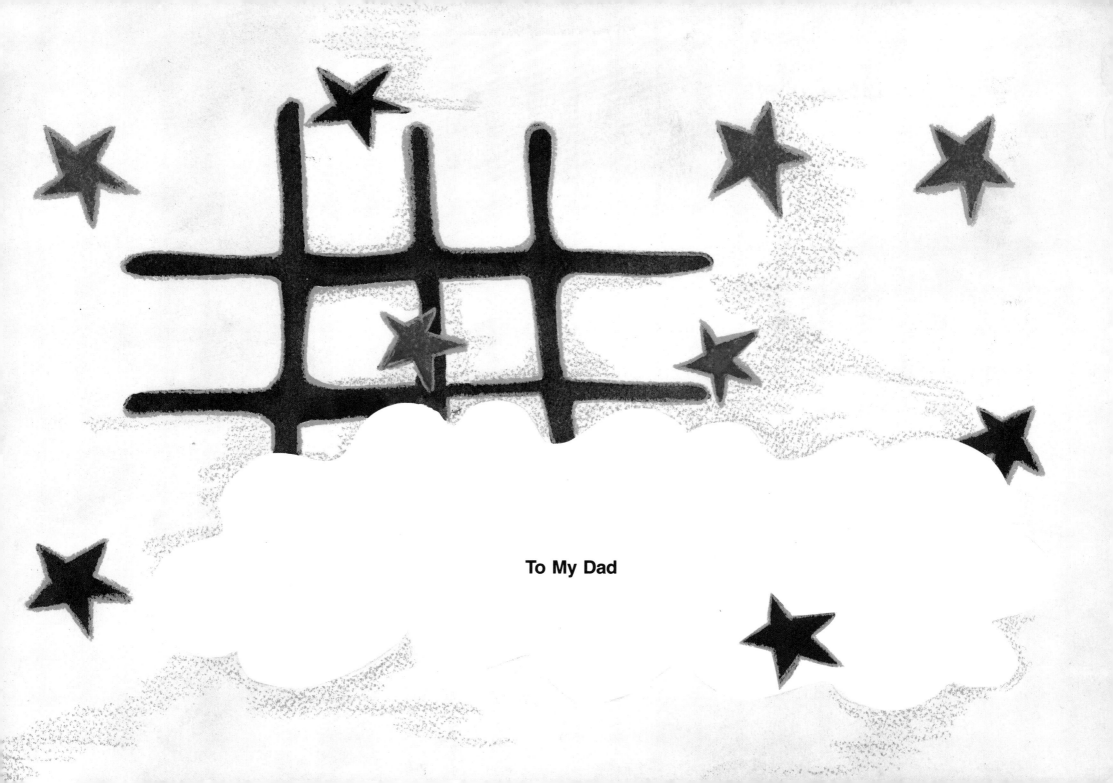

To My Dad

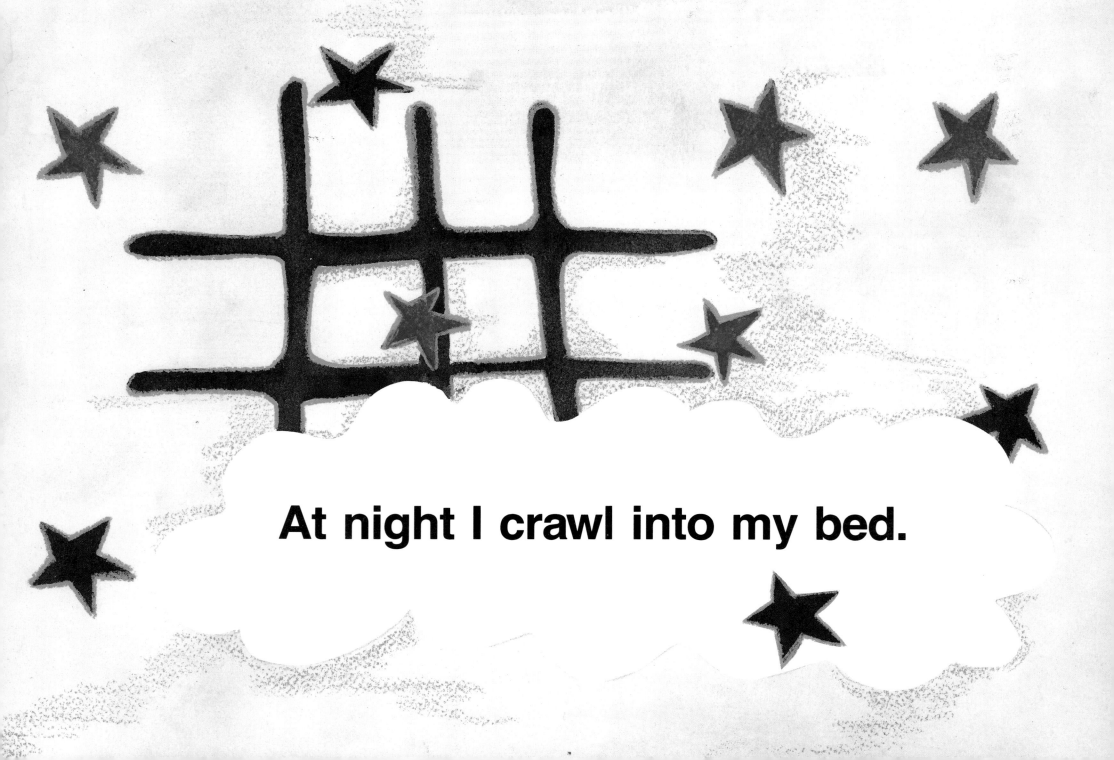

At night I crawl into my bed.

I pull the covers over my head.

To hidden caves
beneath the ground.

To a land that's ruled by gentle beasts.

I join their nightly dance and feast.

The strings sing out
with musical sounds.
The beasts begin
to prance around.

A graceful dance
        seen only by few—
With a rhythm that flows
        and a beat that's new.

I enter the circle—
they step back in awe—

For I am the greatest
dancer of all!

I dance with each beast
one by one,
Leaping and twirling
till we see the sun.

As light begins
        to brighten the land,
We join in a circle,
        hand in hand.

We fall to the ground , we rest and eat fruits and nuts and special treats.

The beasts begin to close their eyes.

I can feel my body rise.

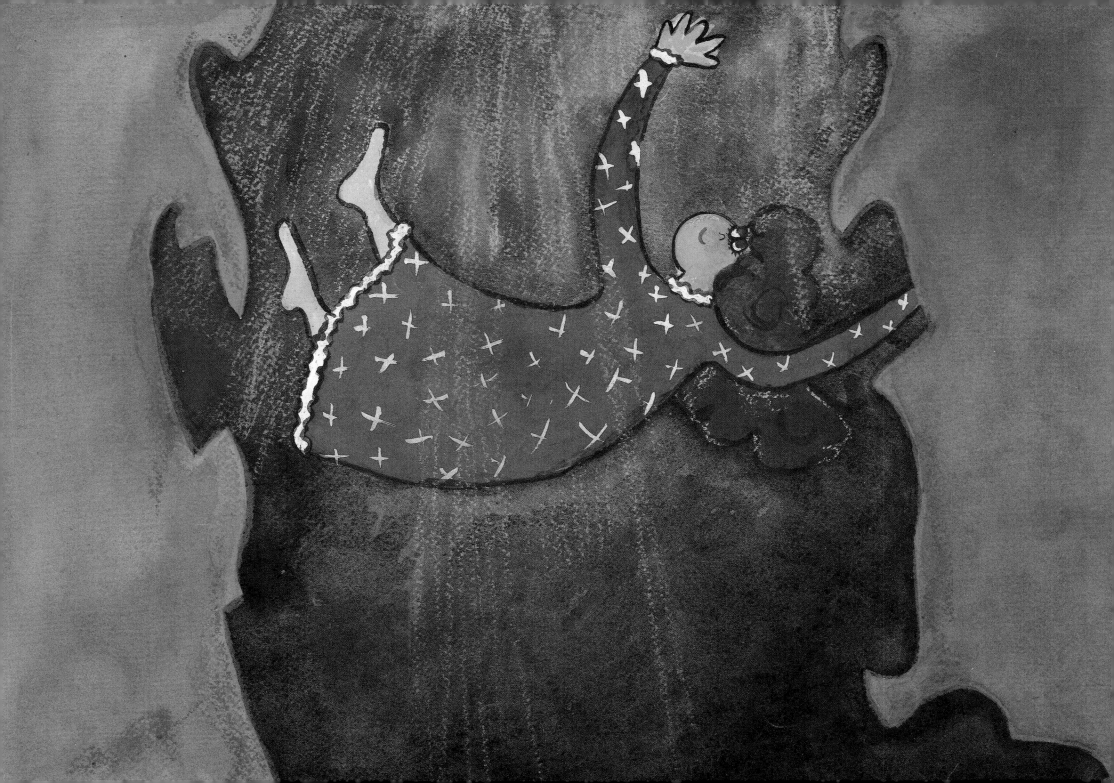

The sun breaks through—
yellow and red.
My pillow is soft
against my head.

I hear the birds singing happy and gay.
I jump out of bed and begin my new day.